Heart of Steel:

A Paranormal Protector Tale

A tale in the Heart of Steel series

DEMELZA CARLTON

IS

ONE

"Promise me, Carline."

Carline pressed her lips together. William couldn't possibly understand what he was asking.

"Carline, if I can't be sure you'll be safe here, then you must come with me."

She blew out a frustrated breath. She'd

accompanied her brother on one of his grain delivery trips downriver to Fremantle, and she'd rather sail back to Britain than do that again. A whole day of the sun beating down on her with no shelter and nothing to do, then a night stuck in a tent with nothing but a thin sheet of canvas between her honour and every drunken lout Britain's colony ships had vomited up on the Swan River's shores.

She was much safer here alone, where the nearest man was on the other side of the river.

"I shall be perfectly safe here, William, I promise," she said. When he opened his mouth to protest, she continued, "At the slightest sign of trouble, I shall take myself up to the mill and lock the door.

I'll load the rifle, take it upstairs and I'll shoot any robber who dares approach."

"Damn right you will. And you don't unlock that door until me or Mr Shenton returns, you hear me?"

"Yes, William," she lied.

"And that's all you'll do. Nothing…nothing else, you hear me?" William said, his voice beginning to shake.

"Yes, William. I hear you," Carline said. Not that a command from him would stop her, if witchcraft was what was needed to protect herself.

"And dress in your boy's garb. Just in case. And if anyone asks…"

"I'm Colin Steel, your brother. I know, William. Truth is, I've worn those breeches more than any of my dresses since we arrived. I'll be needing new ones before long."

A frown creased William's brow. "I know it isn't seemly, but it's to keep you safe, Carline. You do know I do all this because I love you, right?"

She sighed. "Yes, I know. You're the best brother a girl or a boy could ever have. Not many brothers would travel halfway round the world to keep a spinster sister safe. I'll be fine, I promise. You go to Fremantle, take care of business, and bring back fresh supplies so I can cook you a Sunday dinner that isn't stewed kangaroo."

She endured a quarter-hour more of his fussing, before the boat arrived and William was soon too busy loading sacks of flour to do more than wave farewell as the boat headed for the sea.

Carline blew out a breath. William worried too much. But she might as well renew the wards around the mill, just in case. With William gone, she wouldn't have to hide what she was doing to keep him safe.

The sun had barely sunk down behind the trees on the far shore before someone stepped across her wards, sending all her senses tingling. Muttering a curse, she dumped the dishwater on the fire to extinguish it and marched for the mill.

She loaded the rifle, as she'd done a hundred times before, and sank down into the shadows beside the upstairs window.

The first man crept out of the bushes

by the millpond, his body glowing like a ghost with the magic the ward had coated him with when he'd stepped through it. Magic only she could see, of course. The fool didn't know he was lit up like Guy Fawkes.

Carline lined up her shot, then blew out a breath before she fired.

The man dropped.

Two fools jumped out of the bushes, searching for the shooter.

She took them down, too.

One more. The ward had chimed four times, so there was a fourth man somewhere.

Carline loaded the rifle again, then stilled as she thought she'd heard something. There it was again…was there someone at the door?

She peered down, and there he was — shoving at the door as if he meant to enter whether she willed it or no.

"The answer is no, you blackguard," she whispered as she rose to her feet so she could aim straight down.

One, two…

The fourth man dropped.

Only then did Carline dare to breathe again.

The last time someone had attacked the mill, it had been twenty or thirty men, or so Mr Shenton had said. Yet with these four men down, stillness reigned, with no sound but the soft lapping of waves on the riverbank.

If there were thirty men, she would be no match for all of them. She'd need an army of her own to command. Neither she nor William had the money to hire men to guard them, though, and after the poor harvest, Mr Shenton was not flush with cash at the moment, either.

There were magical ways to accomplish the same thing, if she dared…

But no. William would not hear of it.

She waited for perhaps a quarter hour, before she crept downstairs and unbarred the door.

The fourth man lay across the threshold, like a foundation sacrifice of old. A fallen warrior who might rise again if buried here with the right ritual.

If she completed it by morning, William would never know.

Four men was better than one, though, and she did have all night…

What William didn't know wouldn't hurt him. Might even protect him if the mill was attacked again.

Nodding to herself, Carline set to work.

TWO

Foundation sacrifices were way more work than Carline had expected. Just cutting out the first man's heart had taken her more than an hour, and he was the one she'd shot in the chest. The other men took even longer, and there was blood everywhere. She'd have to empty half the millpond to wash it all away when she was done.

She looked longingly at the water, wishing she could wash her blood-slicked self, but a bath would have to wait. She needed to finish the ritual and bury these men by morning, or they would never rise again. They'd just be dead.

Worse, she'd have to explain the bodies to William.

And he'd never leave her alone again.

One more to go, she told herself. She'd already laid the heart-sized chip of foundation stone on the first three men's chests, and the fourth one sat waiting for her to finish the ritual on the final man.

His face looked familiar. Had she met him before? She couldn't remember.

Maybe on the ship…or in passing in Fremantle…

She shook her head. Whoever he had been, he was a dead man now. One who should not have tried to rob the mill, for now he would spend eternity defending it. Serve him right.

She raised her ceremonial blade, and stabbed deep.

"Carline…what…what are you doing?"

William stumbled out of the darkness, his eyes wide as he held his lantern high.

He wasn't meant to be back until morning. He couldn't see this. He wouldn't understand.

She tried to shield the corpse with her body. "It's not what you think, William. These men attacked the mill. I had no choice but to shoot them. They were armed with axes, look." She pointed at the pile of them. English axes, suitable for chopping pine or kindling, or gaining entry into the mill, but no match for the Swan River's mighty hardwoods. More than sharp enough to have ended her if she'd let them swing at her.

Which is why she had not given them that chance. They'd raise their axes in her defence, once she was done.

"Help me dig graves for them, William. Around the walls of the mill," she said. She'd have finished cutting out the final man's heart by the time he was done.

"What have you done?" William hissed. He waved at the final man. "This is Grant Steel, our cousin. And that's

Stanley Steel, another cousin! Carline, you've killed family!"

Family who'd come here to harm her. They wouldn't have triggered the wards if they'd had innocent intentions. But she couldn't tell William that, because then she'd have to admit she'd set the wards, and she'd never hear the end of it.

"I was only defending myself," she said. Well, she had been. Even now, she was trying to protect them.

"No, this is witchcraft, Carline. What you swore you left behind, and would never do again! If anyone here finds out you're a witch…" William swallowed, the shadows making his Adam's apple look even more cadaverous. "We have to bury the bodies."

She nodded. "Yes. Like I said…"

"No, Carline. We need to bury them as far from here as possible. Where no one will find them. But they're family. We can't just bury family in some lonely bush grave. They deserve a proper burial. The least we can do."

A foundation sacrifice was a proper burial, she wanted to scream at him. It was a fitting burial for an enemy. These men might be her cousins, but they weren't family, not like she and William were family. Family protected each other.

William nodded, as if he could read her thoughts. "I'll take them to the burial grounds. No one will notice another grave there, and it's the least we can do for family." He seized the final man beneath his shoulders and heaved.

The man's heart tumbled out of his

chest at Carline's feet.

William didn't notice – he was too busy dragging the body to the boat beside the millpond.

She picked up the heart and dropped it into a bucket with the others.

William carried all four corpses into the boat, then added a shovel and pushed off into the pond. "You get this mess cleaned up. I want there to be no sign they were ever here by the time I come back, you hear?"

Carline started to nod, then stopped as William cursed.

"I have to go up to York in the morning. I came back tonight so I could make an early start. God, Carline, if I hadn't come back early…"

They'd have four immortal warriors to

protect them and William wouldn't have to worry about her again. "William, just listen. If you'll only let me finish…"

"Enough, Carline! This ends now! Clean up this mess or I'll tell the governor myself that you're a witch!"

And she would burn for sure, or perhaps hang. Witches were not welcome in the colonies, any more than they were wanted in Britain. Never mind that her spells had never been for anything but good…

"William, please."

"We will discuss this when I return from York. I may be a few days — Shenton wants me to make sure I have all the agreements in place for next year's harvest, so he can justify building a new mill. Now, be a proper spinster sister and see that my house is in order for when I return, all right?" He offered a weak smile, as if all would be forgiven and forgotten.

Carline slumped. "Yes, William."

If he buried the corpses somewhere, perhaps she could still wake them. She'd just need to know where…

"Good girl."

Better than he would ever know, she thought, as she found a clean bucket to fill with river water to clean up the evidence.

THREE

It must have been close to midnight when the bucket slipped from Carline's aching arms and she didn't have the energy to bend down and pick it up again. She'd deal with what remained of the mess in the morning.

She considered just collapsing on her

bed in the tent that was the closest thing they had to proper accommodation, but the worry that the men she'd killed might have accomplices who'd come looking for them had her turning to the mill instead.

She dragged her things to the upper level, wedged the door shut, and tried to sleep.

But sleep did not come.

Try as she might, the faces of the men she'd killed haunted her, though she could not summon a clear picture of any of them. Perhaps two of them were her cousins, but how was she to know them? There were more than two thousand people in the colony, spread out along hundreds of miles of coastline. William could not possibly have expected her to know them all, let alone have even met them.

She wasn't sure what was worse — attacking and robbing family, or killing them in self defence. If they even were family, for she found it hard to believe that she and William would share blood with such scurrilous thieves.

If they had but asked for her help, her charity, she might have given them some food. But the ward had recognised their ill intentions, and she did not doubt her own magic. She could always trust magic to protect her, while men were questionable at best.

If only she'd succeeded in finishing the ritual. Then she'd have four immortal protectors, instead of just four hearts in a bucket, which she had no idea what to do with.

Wait, hadn't there been a spell that called for kin's heartsblood? It had been one of the darker rituals in the spell book that had been in her family for generations, darker even than foundation sacrifices, for it required not just human sacrifice, but actual communing with the devil, the sort of thing witches had been burned for in centuries past.

Not that it would be likely to work. Carline had never attempted any of the dark rituals before tonight. She'd never so much as cast a curse for a headache before. But now…it wouldn't hurt just to read the ritual, would it? To find out what she might bargain for with magic and the heartsblood of her kinsman?

She leafed through the pages, wishing

she could remember where she'd seen it.

Ah, there it was, squeezed in beside the most horrible drawing of a demon. She usually skipped over that page as quickly as she could, for the great horned dog monster seemed to stare at her, as if he might steal her soul if she only met his gaze for long enough.

Dark stains marred the page – possibly the very heartsblood some long-dead witch had used in the past, and the instructions were hard to read. Carline squinted, struggling to read the old words, and translate them into present-day English.

"To call…no, to summon…a demon…I think it's a demon protector…from the bottom…no, the nether levels of hell, a slave to do the witch's bidding, take a heart, moist with your blood or that of your kin…"

Actually, the spell didn't look that difficult. The bloodied heart needed to be placed in a specially crafted circle, in which the summoned demon must remain until the heart was consumed, at which point it would do her bidding. Kind of like a foundation sacrifice, but instead of an immortal warrior, she'd have a demon protector instead.

With a demon by her side, no one would dare try to rob her ever again.

Well, she had four hearts, enough to try the spell four times. If she failed, then she failed, but if she succeeded…

Before an hour had passed, she had everything assembled on the ground floor of the mill. A dripping heart sat atop the millstone, and the stone itself was circled in salt, then runes written in heartsblood and a ring of lit candles, all surrounded by another circle of salt.

One thing was certain – whether she managed to summon a demon or not, she would be sweeping the floor of the mill thoroughly in the morning.

Now, all she had to do was say the incantation correctly, and a demon should appear, ready to obey her orders and protect her.

Or he'd be so incensed at being dragged here that he'd devour her instantly before returning to hell, and William would never know what she'd done.

Ah, who was she trying to fool? It took a powerful witch to summon anything, let alone a demon, and she had no illusions about her power. The spell would fail, she'd bury the hearts, if they survived the spell, and she'd go upstairs to sleep, or at least attempt to.

Silently, she read the incantation again. Roughly translated, it commanded a demon to enter the circle and agree to fulfil her every desire, until such time as she chose to dismiss him from her service. It seemed like a strange thing to ask for, but she wasn't going to argue with a spell. At least, not until she'd tried and failed to perform it a few times.

"Right, first attempt," Carline said, then took a deep breath and began to read aloud from the book.

Three times she recited the incantation.

And…nothing. Not so much as a wisp of smoke, let alone a big, hulking demon.

Oh, wait, there were some faint words at the bottom of the page she hadn't seen before, so faded it was hard to make them out. They said that the incantation must be repeated as many times as the devil's number, or until the demon appeared.

Wasn't the devil's number 666? She had to repeat the incantation hundreds of times? That would take all night!

She glared at the book. Why did summoning a demon have to be so damned difficult?

She considered sweeping up the whole mess and dumping it in the river. But this was her only chance to perform the ritual. She might not be able to manage it, but she'd never know if she didn't try. And she'd always wonder…

If she couldn't cast a demon, then she'd give up witchcraft altogether, Carline told herself. She'd pretend to be a normal, demure spinster, keeping house for her brother and never use magic again.

He'd like that, wouldn't he? All the men here would. To turn her into a helpless mouse, slaving away as housekeeper and cook and washerwoman and thrice-damned sharpshooter.

She would not be a slave, living in fear any longer. She'd summon a damn demon and he could protect her while she slept.

Carline began the incantation again.

Over and over she repeated it, until she no longer had to look at the book to remember words that would forever resonate on her tongue.

"I command thee, demon…"

"I command thee!"

"I command thee, demon, to enter this circle…"

"I command thee…"

Fury drove her, charging her limbs with energy she knew not where it came from. If she couldn't summon a simple demon, then what sort of witch was she? She should have stayed home and married an apothecary, or even a simple labourer, and she'd be living in a house with a roof right now, instead of sleeping in a tent on sand, halfway around the world in this godforsaken place full of snakes and giant hopping kangaroos and spiders as big as her hand and…

Wait, was that a shadow atop the millstone? Growing larger, like smoke rising from a fire, only she'd never seen a fire that large outside bonfire night, or so much smoke…

Carline finished the incantation, and began again, but there was too much smoke, reaching down her throat and trying to choke her. Couldn't…breathe…

Darkness seized her, crushing the air from her lungs and stealing the very thoughts from her head until she knew no more.

FOUR

"I command thee, demon, to enter this circle..."

Exhilaration took his breath away as the mop almost slipped from his hands. A summons! Oh, a summons!

He couldn't remember how long it had been since he'd last been called up to the surface for a reprieve from Hell. It seemed like he'd been cleaning Level Eight for an eternity, waiting for just this sort of opportunity. Finally, it had come.

He raced to be the first to the portal. It was already glowing with the power of the summoner's spell. When it reached its peak, the blindingly bright portal would be visible from even the highest levels of Hell, and every demon, hellspawn and damned soul would be headed for it, and the freedom it offered.

Already a fight had broken out between two hellspawn and an imp. Three more imps sat atop a hellhound on the other side of the cavern, wagering on the outcome and launching fireballs at the combatants.

"Did you hear who or what the summoner wants?" he asked the imps.

The imps sniggered. "Fulfilment of desire. Must be a virgin summoner. We should send the hellhound through. That'll teach them not to be specific."

"Send me. I can do far more damage than any hellhound," he said.

The imps exchanged glances, before one said, "Win the brawl with those two, and it's all yours."

Two? Hadn't there been three?

He blinked. The imp had left the fray, to double over laughing on the ground while the two hellspawn, a male and a female, continued fighting. She'd taken the form of a harpy, and she'd sunk her claws deep into the male's back, tearing out chunks of flesh in her quest to rip out his heart. The short, stocky male, twice as broad as he was tall, was armed with a barbed whip, which he was busily flailing over his shoulder to tear at any part of the harpy he could reach. Streaks of blood ran down her cheeks, and one of her wings was sliced to ribbons, yet still she fought on. Whoever made it through the portal to answer the summons would get a brand new body, so all she had to do was survive the fight, however grievously injured she might be.

If he'd had more time, he'd let the two tear each other apart, then walk past their dying bodies to enter the portal, but the light was growing brighter, every moment he waited, and the eager war cries of the horde descending grew ever louder.

Good thing he'd chosen the body of a hulking winged devil, formed in the image of Lucifer himself, to better endure the heavy labours of Level Eight.

He snapped the mop handle across his thigh, and advanced on the fighting pair.

With arms bulked with muscle from carrying corpses, he yanked the two apart, shaking off the blood that showered over him from their wounds as he dropped them both on the floor. The shorter length of mop handle went through the harpy's throat, silencing her shrieks. The longer length, with the mop head still attached, he drove through the male's stocky chest, until the point scraped against the stone floor below. The male spat blood at him. "I wanted to taste human flesh. So sweet…" His words faded as his corpse did.

At least he wouldn't have to clean these two up — they'd get new bodies when the next day dawned. Such was the undying existence of a hellspawn.

The way to the portal was clear. Not for long…

"To the victor go the spoils!" the imps cackled, before they all rolled around laughing. "Go, before more arrive, and the devil's own luck to you, Spawn of Lilith!"

He hesitated. The devil's own luck was the worst kind anyone could wish him, and he well knew it.

"What do you mean by that?" he asked, squaring up to fight the imps, too, if he must.

"Here they come!" The imps were on their feet now, a smoking fireball in each hand.

It was now or never, ill luck or no. He dived for the portal, with half a dozen flying fireballs on his tail.

FIVE

The cool kiss of a surface breeze across his skin was as close to heaven as he'd ever been. But he didn't have even a moment to savour it, for the fireballs came through the portal an instant after he did, and he was forced to flatten himself against the floor to avoid becoming their target.

The fireballs splashed against the walls instead, setting the place ablaze with light. A virgin summoner, indeed – no one with any experience in dark magic would summon a demon inside.

He rose, peering about for the summoner.

Oh, by Lucifer's left testicle, a true virgin indeed – a maiden witch, clutching a grimoire to her chest, as she coughed in the smoke already clouding the air. Even as he watched, she swooned, and would have hit the burning wall behind her if he hadn't raced over to catch her first.

No way was he letting his first summoning in centuries end with his new mistress dying seconds after he'd appeared. No, he intended to stay here, as far from Hell as possible, for as long as she'd have him. But first, he had to get her out of this inferno, for the fierce blaze had reached the roof, and the whole structure would come down soon enough.

She was a tiny thing, cradled against his chest, but he didn't make the mistake of thinking she was weak. She'd summoned him from Hell, hadn't she? And try as he might, he couldn't pry that grimoire from her fingers.

He carried her outside into the night air, looking for somewhere he might safely lay her down. The ground in all directions was a muddy quagmire, looking like the Third Level of Hell. Well, except there were no damned souls or three-headed dogs to contend with. Just the cool night air and the swish of waves on a dark shore.

He searched for higher ground, somewhere that might be dry, and that's where his luck kicked in. On the hill overlooking their present position stood a tent, glowing ghostly white in the moonlight. This must be his maiden mistress's bedchamber, and that's where he would take her, and wait for her to wake up, so that he could grant her every desire.

SIX

When Carline woke, her mouth and throat burned like she'd been eating hot ash. Oh, damn, she'd been trying to summon a demon in the mill, and she must have somehow passed out. She was lucky she hadn't hit her head on anything on the way down.

She tried to sit up, but the pounding in her head forced her back down, where the pain was only bearable if she lay flat, squinting up at the canvas tent.

That couldn't be right. William must have come back and brought her here, which meant he'd seen the mess in the mill, and…

"I can explain," she croaked.

"Explain what, mistress?"

That wasn't William's voice. It was deeper, and darker, like treacle poured over gravel and boulders. Not the voice of anyone she'd ever heard, for she'd remember a voice she could feel in her very bones.

She dared to turn her head, to glimpse…

"Oh God."

Carline squeezed her eyes shut, but it

was too late. She'd seen the picture of the monster in the book, brought to life, but on a much, much bigger scale than she'd imagined.

"No, mistress, I am not so high. Just your demon, as ordered."

She wished she could remember. There'd been that shadow, and some smoke, and then…she'd woken up here, with a monster leaning over her.

"How did I get here?" she demanded.

He ducked his head, which gave her a better look at his horns. Curled, like a ram's, but wickedly sharp on the ends.

"I carried you, mistress. The…building we were in caught fire, from the fires of Hell that came through with me, and the smoke overcame you. I've been waiting for you to wake up so that you could tell me what you desire."

A monster asking about her desires. Carline felt hysterical laughter bubbling up, but she forced it down. Best not to let the demon think she was mad.

Unless she was mad, and she was only imagining the demon. He did bear an uncanny resemblance to the drawing in her book.

"I desire you to move away from me. Your appearance is quite frightening," she said.

His brow furrowed. "I am not as you desire, mistress? Tell me what you desire, and I will endeavour to please."

His eyes pierced hers, and it felt like he was delving into her soul. Or doing something to her insides, at any rate.

Without ever breaking her gaze, he began to change. His enormous brow, and the horns upon it, began to shrink, along with his doglike snout, until his face looked almost human. His skin warmed from deep grey to tan, like a labourer who spent all day in the sun, working hard to develop so many muscles on top of muscles. She'd never seen a man in such a state of undress, and it was doing twisty things to her insides, lower down than before.

"Is this form more to your taste, mistress?" he asked. There was less gravel in his voice, but he'd replaced it with treacle. If anything, his new tone resonated even more with her bones than before.

And why was her mouth so dry? "My mouth tastes of ash and smoke," she said, avoiding his question.

He bowed his head. "Then I shall fetch you a drink, mistress."

He returned with a pannikin of William's medicinal brandy, as if, once again, he'd read her thoughts. Carline drank it down in three gulps.

Her throat still burned, but in a good way this time.

"What is your name, demon?" she asked.

He shook his head. "I do not have a name, mistress."

"Everyone has a name. The other demons must call you something," Carline persisted.

"I am a hellspawn, mistress, one of thousands of the progeny of Lilith and Lucifer, all birthed at the same time to serve in Hell. Mostly, they call all of us Spawn, for one of us is the same as another to the senior demons. They have names, like Lord Lucifer and Lilith and

Geryon and Ananiel, but not us."

Pity smote her hard, and it took her a long moment before she could think of what to say to that. No names. One of thousands. She couldn't even begin to imagine…

"Well, I can't you call you Spawn. That means a child, and a big, fierce demon like you is most definitely not a child," she said.

He grinned. "No, mistress, the form of your desires is most pleasing indeed. Such strength and power is almost like the form I prefer in Hell."

She almost didn't dare to ask, but curiosity won. "What do you usually look like, then?"

He waved at his body. "Much the same as this, mistress, only with wings."

"Show me." The words were out

before she'd really thought them through.

And so were his wings, great leathery things that barely fitted in the tent, with sharp bone spurs jutting from the joints.

"Can I touch them?" she breathed.

"I am yours to command, mistress. You summoned me, after all." He angled his wing so all she had to do was reach out and touch it. Soft, like the finest kid leather, and warm, from the heat of his body. Her insides did that twisty thing again as she imagined touching more of him, to see if demon skin was as soft as his wings.

He dropped to his knees beside her, and spread his arms wide. "How would you like me to pleasure you first, mistress?"

SEVEN

"What do you mean?" Carline demanded.

The demon's face lit up with a smile that made him look more like an angel than one of hell's denizens. "Oh, you truly are a virgin summoner! I can't remember the last time I served someone so innocent. You summoned me to be your paramour, mistress, to fulfil your desires. If you seek a pleasurable deflowering, you have definitely summoned the right demon for that! Why, I myself have been deflowered so many times, by so many summoners, I've put together the perfect, most painless way to initiate a girl into the full bloom of her femininity. In fact..."

"That's not possible! You can't possibly be...deflowered...more than once. Once you've lost your flower, it's gone! And you're a man. Men can't...they don't have the parts..." Oh, she was blushing. She could feel her cheeks burning. If William could hear her now, he'd think she'd gone mad, speaking of such things. She wasn't sure he'd be wrong, either.

The demon chuckled, a low rumbling that did things to her insides. "Oh, mistress, for humans perhaps it is so, but for demons it is very, very different. A body can be deflowered but once, yet every time a demon is summoned, we take on the form our summoner desires. So if the master desires a sweet young maiden, then for him, I am a sweet young maiden, until he sends me back to Hell. Then he has but to summon me back again, and I appear in a new body, exactly as he desires. In fact, there was a particular brothel madam who was also an accomplished witch, and she would summon us for her clients, the ones who would pay a premium for that sort of purity that is rarely found in a brothel."

Carline's head was spinning. "Stop, please, stop. Am I to understand that you are a demon, and I summoned you, and that you have no form or name except those I choose to give you?"

The demon gave a nod.

"But…but…" Carline searched for the book, seized it, flipped furiously through the pages, then held out the one with the summoning spell on it. "But look! I summoned a protector, not a paramour! It says nothing here about any of this!" She held the book out so that he might see the truth for himself.

The demon took the book delicately in his huge hands, shaking his head. "Mistress, I can see the likeness of a hellhound on the page, much as I first appeared to you, but none of these symbols mean much of anything to me. Reading is for senior demons and those who have a need for it. I am just a lowly hellspawn, made for manual labour and whatever base tasks Hell and those who summon me deem me fit for."

She seized the book and pointed at the words, reading them aloud so that he would understand. "See? It says to summon a demon protector, I must repeat this incantation while standing outside the triple-spelled circle around my kinsman's heartsblood."

He shook his head. "Mistress, whoever wrote such things in your book was wrong. This incantation here, the one where you command a demon to come and fulfil your desire, without naming the demon…well, those are the words for bringing you a paramour. I've heard them often enough, for it is the only incantation a lowly hellspawn can answer. My only chance of leaving Hell, if for a little while. So I know those words like a blessing from Heaven, mistress, and to have the pleasure of answering your summons…as you command me, I will do whatever you ask. Anything, so that I might stay here a little longer. Any pleasure you desire, you have but to name it, and I shall give it to you." He fell to his knees, his thigh muscles bulging beneath his weight.

One leg was easily as wide as she was, Carline thought. Sitting on his lap would be as spacious as any chair, and if he wrapped those strong arms around her…she knew she'd be safe. No one else would be able to touch her.

"What is your command, mistress?" he rumbled.

"Protect me," she said. "Protect me from all the unscrupulous men in this colony, who would take me or my brother's property for their own. Protect me from those who would harm me, and I shall keep you at my side, far from Hell, for as long as it is within my power."

"Until you dismiss me, or one of us dies, mistress. That's how a summoning usually works," he said .

Carline nodded. "Very well. Protect me, and you may stay as long as I live."

He bowed low. "It will be my pleasure, mistress."

EIGHT

All that first day, and well into the night, Carline lost count of the number of times she'd caught herself staring at the demon as he stood guard or patrolled Mr Shenton's borders. He'd fashioned himself a sort of loincloth out of a bit of burned cloth he'd salvaged from the ashes that were all that remained of the mill, and that's all he wore as he scattered ash over the remaining bloodstains she hadn't managed to wash away last night.

So when Captain Ellis from the Regiment rowed into the millpond to ask after her welfare, she was able to tell a coherent tale about falling asleep in the mill with a candle burning, and knocking it over in her sleep. If not for the quick thinking of the mill's new labourer – she gestured in the demon's direction – she might have burned along with the mill. All the labourer's possessions and even his clothes had been consumed by the blaze, while the poor man had laboured half the night to put the fire out.

Of course, then the demon had chosen that moment to come over to join the conversation, which necessitated introductions. Mr Hellspawn was hardly a name she could tell Captain Ellis, and somehow her stumbling tongue had turned it into Mr Bell, Sean Bell. "This is Captain Ellis, captain of the Regiment," she finished, hoping the men would shake hands and be done with it.

The demon summoned a warm smile and a hearty handshake for the captain. "A pleasure, Captain Ellis. Any friend of the mistress is a friend of mine."

Carline frowned. "My name is Miss Steel, Sean, and you must call me that. I am no man's mistress." She wished her cheeks did not heat at the very thought of it. Perhaps it was the demon's doing, making her blush, standing there looking like a near-naked man with all those muscles on top of muscles.

The demon ducked his head. "Yes, Miss Steel. Of course, Miss Steel."

Captain Ellis's gaze slid from Carline to the demon and back again, as if he could read her thoughts and he didn't approve. Of course he didn't. Men could lust after women and treat them like property, but for a woman to even have a lustful thought about a man, however innocent, was far too dangerous to be borne.

"Mr Bell, in light of you losing all your things helping Miss Steel here, I'm sure we can find you some clothes as might fit. One of the men in the Regiment must have something that will fit you. I'll see to it directly." Without another word, he turned on his heel and headed back to his boat.

When the man was halfway across the river, and well out of earshot, she dared to speak again. "You can't tell anyone what you are, or where you came from. If anyone finds out I summoned a demon, they'll burn me or hang me for sure, and you'll get sent back to Hell. They must think you're a normal human labourer."

The demon beamed. "Oh, yes, Miss Steel. Mr Sean Bell, as you have named me. My first ever, respectable human name. It fairly trips off the tongue, too. Sean. Mr Sean Bell. It will give me a thrill of pleasure every time I hear you say it, mistress. I mean…Miss Steel." He dropped his voice to a whisper. "It has other benefits, too. Should I be killed in your service and sent back to Hell, you now have a name with which to summon me. So instead of summoning any demon, you may be certain I will come when you call."

He bowed, then returned to his patrol.

Carline watched him, those muscles moving in his legs with every easy stride, arms pumping and flexing all those muscles in his back that she'd never really noticed on a man before, but now couldn't take her eyes off him.

Summon him again? Hell, she still wasn't sure how she'd managed to summon him once. And the thought of him dying in her service, even if he was protecting her…no, she did not even want to think about it. No, Mr Sean Bell, formerly hellspawn demon, wasn't going anywhere if she had any say in it.

Oh, and there he was, coming out of the bushes and marching toward her this time. Those chest muscles and the ripples down his belly…why, they were almost hypnotic. It certainly took her a long moment after he'd passed her to get the image out of her head and remember what she'd been doing.

NINE

He marched through her dreams, wearing nothing but a loincloth, though Captain Ellis had brought shirts and trousers and boots for him. He had horns, too, which tangled in her hair when he kissed her, as he pressed that hard, muscled body against hers. She wore nothing but a thin nightgown, which he tore off her with one swipe of his claws before his hands fastened over her breasts, squeezing gently as her breath caught in her throat at anyone touching her in so intimate a place.

Then his hand slid lower, down her belly and between her legs, to an even more secret place. The heat of his hand invading her, even as she welcomed him inside, opening her legs wider…until a sort of explosion of pleasure rocked through her, blowing her apart even as she screamed for joy…

"Miss Steel, Miss Steel! What is it you desire?"

She opened her eyes to find the demon – Sean – leaning over her, his eyes reflecting the flame from the lantern he held.

You, naked and in my bed, she wanted to say, but she didn't dare. Thank Heaven it had only been a dream.

"Nothing, Sean, nothing. I was asleep," she said instead.

He frowned. "But you called my name, Miss Steel. Shouted it with such urgency, I could not resist your summons. I can smell your arousal, Miss Steel — is it pleasure you desire? Tell me, and I shall give it to you all night, if that is your wish."

"Don't be ridiculous. I'm not married, and I will stay a virgin until I marry, or until I die, as is proper. I couldn't possibly do such a thing. It's just not done."

The demon laughed softly. "Miss Steel,

I assure you, I have known many virtuous virgins who have experienced a great deal of pleasure, before ever reaching the marriage bed. Why, there are a thousand ways to pleasure a woman, an old eunuch once told me, and most of them leave no trace, except for the smile on her face and the rapid beating of her heart. In fact, I once tried over nine hundred of them with a Vestal Virgin, who died virgo intacta. I can show you, if you like."

Nine hundred? Good God, what in Heaven's name could he mean?

"I am yours to command, Miss Steel," he reminded her.

She wanted…she wanted so much to say yes, but she didn't dare.

Instead, Carline shook her head.

"Sean, I need you to protect me, or I will not be able to sleep. Please, do not speak of such things. I dare not even think of them."

He bowed his head. "As you wish, Miss Steel."

And he was gone.

Leaving her daring to wonder how there could possibly be nine hundred ways to pleasure a virgin woman, when she couldn't even think of ten…

TEN

"Miss Steel! You called for me. What would you have me do?"

Carline opened her eyes and gasped. This time, her dream had gone much, much further. She'd taken Sean into her bed and he'd…she'd…and…she wasn't even sure married couples did THAT.

But oh, how much she wanted to…

"I need you to protect me, Sean," she managed to say, her voice choked up with all the words she wanted to say but didn't dare. She needed him to protect her from herself and all the sinful thoughts and desires as well as anyone else who might arrive and mean her harm.

"I am protecting you, Miss Steel. In fact, the moment someone crosses your wards, I shall race out and challenge them, defending you with my life, but I can do that from anywhere on the property. From down by the millpond…or right here, in your tent, where I can watch over you, if you wish it."

Watch her as she writhed in her sleep, soaking through her drawers, as she moaned his name? Hell, no, she could not bear it. That would be almost as bad as giving in to her desires, and allowing him to share her bed…

"I can't," she wailed.

Sean dropped to his knees beside her, then placed his hands on either side of her waist as he leaned over her. "You can, because you wish for this as ardently as I do. I can sense your desires, as I take the form to best satisfy them."

Oh God, he even had his horns back — the ones she'd dreamed about holding in her hands as he…as he…

He slid her drawers down her legs and tossed them aside.

She whimpered, wishing she had the fortitude to say no when every bit of her being screamed YES.

"Do you truly want me to tear off your

nightgown?" he asked.

He'd done so in her dreams, but she didn't own many, and good linen was hard to come by in the colony, so Carline reluctantly lifted the garment over her head and tossed it aside.

Naked as the day she was born, she couldn't…she couldn't…

"Come and sit in my lap, Miss Steel."

He'd shifted to sit in the chair beside her bed, and he patted his lap. At least he was still wearing pants, not naked like he'd been in her dreams.

Hesitantly, she perched on his knee.

Strong hands seized her waist, spinning her around to face him so she sat astride his lap, instead of sidesaddle. She could feel the heat and hardness of him between her legs, even through his trousers.

"Take hold of my horns," he commanded, ducking his head.

They were as hot and hard as the rest of him, the ridges making them very easy to hold on to.

"Now ride me, Miss Steel, ride me hard, like I know you want to."

Heat rushed to her cheeks, to her belly, to every bit of her, as she wanted to but didn't dare. Oh, how could he know such a thing?

"You summoned me to fulfil your desires, Miss Steel, and I know your desires better than even you do."

Oh God oh God oh God…

The demon's hands seized her hips and ground her against him, back and forth, as she hung on for dear life. Then he fastened his lips around her nipple and began to suck. A bolt of lightning seemed to shoot through her, from her breast to the very core of her.

"Sean…oh, Sean…" she sobbed, lost in the sensation. Not even in her dreams had anything felt this good.

"Ride harder, Miss Steel. Faster."

The rough fabric between her legs, the hot hardness beneath, rubbing faster and faster against the tenderest, most private parts of her…

Carline was going to fly apart, cleft in two by the heat between her thighs. His wicked, wicked heat…

And then she screamed his name, and nothing would ever be the same again.

ELEVEN

Carline woke in the faint predawn light, with Sean's strong arms securing her against his chest. Safe. Protected. Sated. Oh, what a blissful night. She only wished she could stay in bed with him forever.

"Miss Steel, I must beg a favour from

you. Before the clear light of day brings with it the regrets and realisations that tend to come with a harsh awakening, I wish to pleasure you one more time. So that if you choose to dismiss me from your service after last night, at least I will know whether you taste as good as you smell. Permit me to pleasure you again, Miss Steel."

His hands stroked her thighs, and she opened for him, ready and eager for whatever he wanted to do to her next.

"Will you permit me, Miss Steel?"

"Oh, yes." She was surprised at how breathless with want the words came out. Had one night in Sean's arms turned her into a wanton? And yet, she was a virgin still, or so Sean assured her.

Strokes became kisses, as he lifted her

legs over his shoulders. He inhaled deeply, then met her gaze. "You smell so sweet, I can scarcely resist a moment longer." His tongue flicked out, long and forked, and licked his lips. "Take hold of my horns, Miss Steel."

She obeyed.

And then he impaled her with his tongue.

First she whimpered, then she moaned, and as his fingers went to work on her in perfect harmony with his sinful tongue, her breath caught in her throat, unable to escape, as she felt a pleasurable explosion building within her, one she could not, would not stop, for sensation had started to overwhelm her.

Send him away? She wanted to keep Sean in her bed forever, and never leave the sheets herself.

She heard her voice scream his name, but she was too lost in her own blessed release to care what sounds she made. And Sean…Sean did not stop, his fingers already working her quivering body to another precipitous cliff from which she had no choice but to fall into bliss.

Once, twice, three times, she screamed his name, before he gave her trembling lady parts one final, languorous lick and said, "You have the sweetest juices I have ever tasted, Miss Steel. If I could but taste them every morning of my life, and hear you scream my name for joy, I would consider myself in Heaven."

"Yes," she said, still holding tight to his horns, for she did not want to let go. "If you wake me so every morning, I will never want to send you away, as long as I live."

He tugged his horns from her hands, wiping his mouth with the back of his hand. "So I am to protect you another day, Miss Steel?"

"Forever, Sean," she vowed.

TWELVE

Every night, Carline fell asleep in Sean's arms, and every morning she woke to his kisses on her thighs. Protector and paramour, all in one…she wished she'd summoned a demon long ago, for she'd never felt so well-protected, so safe, so loved. And it would never grow old, for every night he surprised her with new ways to bring her pleasure, leaving her breathless for more.

Until one night she woke in darkness, well before dawn, with Sean's hand over her mouth.

She recognised the tingling of alarm coursing through her body a moment later.

The wards. Someone had tripped the wards. Someone was here, and they meant her harm.

She scrambled to dress in boy's clothes, while Sean, still wearing his trousers, slipped out into the night.

Carline didn't dare light a lantern, so she had to load the rifle by touch in the dark. She prayed she would not have to fire it, for God only knew if she'd loaded it right. Perhaps the sight of a rifle aimed at him would be enough to scare the intruder away.

Or that Sean would take care of him, and she wouldn't have to shoot anyone.

She dashed out of the tent, straight into his arms.

Only these arms were not Sean's, winding tight around her like seaweed, dragging her against his skinny body. Hands pried the rifle from her fingers before she could even think to aim it at anyone.

"Now, a gun's a dangerous toy for a boy. I'll take that, son."

The one holding her gave her a shake. "This one's no boy, sir, even if she is dressed like one in weskit and trousers. I can feel her dugs right through her weskit." His fingers dug into her breast until she cried out in pain.

"A girl, is it? Mebbe the mistress of the mill, who Ellis said might be more accommodating than the man who owns the mill upriver?" A hand grabbed her chin and tilted her face up to meet his in the light of the lantern he'd uncovered. "She's a plain one, that's for sure. Eh, miller's wife, what say you to a deal? You give us the provisions we need, and no one needs to get hurt."

Carline stomped on the foot of the brute holding her, then kicked him in the shins, hard enough to make him release her. "Sean, Sean, help!" she shouted.

But Sean did not appear, and the two men soon captured her again.

"Ellis said the husband's gone upriver,

so who's the fellow she's shouting to, eh?"

"Tricksy minx must be shouting at the neighbours, or trying to affright us into thinking the husband is home." He shook her until her teeth ached. "No more of this silliness, wench. Now, who else is here at the mill with you?"

"Sean, the general labourer. He's the size of an ox, with the strength of one, too, and if he sees you threatening me, he'll gore you and trample you like an angry bull, and no mistake. If I were you, I'd run away, as fast as you are able, and leave us alone!" Carline snapped.

The blow came out of nowhere, colliding with her cheek so hard she feared he'd broken it.

"Enough of your bluster. We need

flour, and you're going to give it to us, and we're not paying six shillings a pound like the other miller tried to charge us. Now, where is this man of yours, so he can load the flour into the boat for us?" He raised his voice. "Sean, your mistress needs you! Come out, nice and slow and easy, and she won't get hurt. For if you hide in the bushes, planning an ambush or some such thing, we'll get bored, and we'll be looking to your mistress to entertain us. But if you help us, maybe we'll give you a taste of the mistress, too. You'd like that, wouldn't you? Not enough women in this colony – but a free turn with the miller's wife has to beat poking some pox-ridden whore!"

Carline's blood froze in her veins.

God, she'd spent so much of her life trying to protect her honour, and here was a pair of ruffians, trading her body and her maidenhead as if she were their property. It wasn't to be borne.

She'd rather have given her body to Sean, for at least he'd have given her pleasure in equal measure to his own.

If she got out of this alive, she would take Sean for her paramour, she promised herself.

"For six shillings a pound, that other miller ought to have offered us his wife. Might have sweetened the deal a little."

"I like this deal better. We take all the flour here, and our pleasure of the miller's wife, and we let her live."

"But what if she tells someone what we did, sir?"

"Oh, she won't be telling anything to anyone. For if she does, we'll come back to silence her. And no one would believe her, anyway. We'll say we paid for the flour and the tumble in her bed, and if she can't show her husband the money, well, likely she's spent it on whatever fripperies women like her want. No fault of ours."

"That's clever, sir."

The man carrying the lantern straightened his shoulders, as if he felt the weight of the other man's compliment.

"Now, how about the missus here and I get started while we wait for that labourer to wake up. Better get that waistcoat off, so I can see your titties, missus." Long, thin fingers scrabbled at the buttons of her waistcoat.

Carline struggled, but the other man held her fast. There was nowhere to go.

"Sean!" she screamed.

The two men only laughed. Neither of them made any move to silence her, as if they either didn't expect Sean to hear them, or they simply didn't care.

"Those titties are tiny! Scarcely even a handful! Are you sure she's not a boy?"

"Get her trousers off, sir, and then we'll see if she has a notch or a prick."

Carline screamed again.

THIRTEEN

Sean headed for the water, where he knew the men had crossed Miss Steel's ward. Sure enough, there were three men and a boat, all standing around as if they were waiting for something.

Sean grinned. They might not know it, but they were waiting for their doom, in the shape of him. A hellspawn, to be precise.

He took the first one by surprise, knocking him out with a single punch. The other two saw their comrade fall and turned to defend against their attacker. One drew out a blade, while the other shakily drew a pistol.

The pistol-wielder was nearer. Sean unfolded his wings, and launched himself at the man, knocking both man and pistol to the ground. Except…the man didn't hit the ground first, for there was water in the way. He went under with Sean on top of him, and Sean bore down with all his weight, keeping the man under the surface until he was forced to breathe river water. Precious seconds passed until the man went limp, and the last man was almost upon him, blade dangerously close to Sean's wings.

Only his fear at fighting a demon kept the man at bay, and Sean knew he didn't have long.

The pistol glinted in the moonlight, and Sean seized it, bringing the muzzle to bear on the man.

Up went his hands, along with the blade.

Giving Sean a clean shot, which of course he took. He might be a demon, but he was no fool. The last man, shot in the head, went into the water with his companions.

Only then did he hear Miss Steel's scream.

Not a scream of joy, like the others he'd been responsible for, but a scream of fear.

There were more than three men, and

one of them was even now threatening Miss Steel.

Pistol in one hand, blade in the other, Sean charged through the bush.

One of the brutes held Miss Steel's arms tight behind her, while the other was busily trying to unfasten her trousers. Her vest hung unbuttoned, baring her breasts for all to see.

The pistol and the blade fell from his fingers. He was Miss Steel's demon protector, and they would feel a demon's wrath.

With a flap of his wings, Sean took to the air.

FOURTEEN

Carline closed her eyes. Perhaps if she swooned, she would not remember this. This stranger's hands on her flesh, his foul breath in her ear, the eagerness that lit his eyes with an unholy light…

A chill breeze blew across her breasts, sending her shivering. The hands fumbling at her trousers pulled away, as if he'd decided to pull out a knife to tear the cloth instead of undoing the buttons.

Please, no.

Then the man holding her stepped away, so instead of his rapid heartbeat against her back, all she could feel was his hands gripping her wrists, until those, too, let go.

Hands landed on her shoulders. Bigger, warmer, stronger than any part of her attackers.

"Sean?" she whispered, hardly daring to hope.

"Are you all right, Miss Steel? Did they hurt you?"

She started to shake her head, then winced as her bruised cheek twinged. "Only a little. Are they…?"

"No, wait…"

She opened her eyes, hoping to see the men down on their knees before her, with Sean standing over them. Instead, she saw…a leg, ripped off at the knee, lying beside a head that looked like it had been torn off. Two arms lay on the ground behind her, like some sort of gory cross a last ditch defender had made in a desperate attempt to save his soul. The rest of the man lay in a heap, his chest ripped open to expose what had once been his heart and lungs, before Sean's claws had shredded them.

"Miss Steel, avert your eyes. This is a normal day's work for Level Eight in Hell, and I'll have it cleaned up in no time."

But she couldn't look away. The men who'd intended to rob and rape her were no more. Sean had done a far more efficient job than she had, either time she'd been attacked. He took the bodies down to the river, where the men had dragged a boat up on the shore, and added these pieces to the three corpses already lying below the gunwales. Then he rowed the vessel out into the current. As the boat began to move downriver, he leaped up, wings catching the air, as he brandished an axe. Once, twice, three times, he struck, until the boat started to sink. Only then did Sean head back to shore, to her.

"Come back to the tent, where you can sleep," Sean said. "I'll finish cleaning up, so in the morning, no one will ever know they were here."

But Carline could not sleep. She watched Sean sweep the ground, with all the efficiency of a man who dealt with blood and gore every day. Was that what his life was like in Hell, that had him so eager to come up here? Even if he was summoned to satisfy men's darkest desires? Much like those two dead men had tried to do to her.

She and Sean were similar souls – both slaves to others' wants and whims, never allowed to give in to their own desires, to live their own lives.

He'd saved her life, and she owed him...everything. First and foremost, she would do everything in her power to keep him here, with her, and far from Hell.

He returned from the millpond, dripping wet as if he'd dunked his whole body in the water. Water trickled down his muscles, glittering in the moonlight.

She could have died tonight. It was

only because of Sean that she still stood here. A man, a demon, a hero.

"Let me take you to bed, Miss Steel, where I promise I'll keep you safe," he said, holding out his arms.

FIFTEEN

Sean lifted her up, marvelling at how light she felt in his arms. He'd never met a human woman who could look at carnage with such a calm mien. Oh, he knew demons who could do it, but Miss Steel was a human witch, a witch so tender-hearted she'd given him a name, and a form so like his own that it was like she'd read his desires, instead of him reading hers, as was expected.

She wrapped her arms around his neck, tugging his head down. He didn't realise her intentions until her lips met his for a kiss, her tongue dancing with his as though she meant to seduce him.

Sean fought back a laugh. She didn't need to seduce him – she had only to ask, and he would do whatever she commanded. He had to admit, though, that he'd never served a summoner he was half as willing to obey as Miss Steel.

"Take me to bed, Sean. I'm tired. Tired of being a virtuous spinster, a virgin at everyone's whim but my own. And then, when you have shattered my maidenhead into a million pieces, I want you to tell me your desires, and we'll see if I can grant one of those."

He didn't believe what he was hearing. That wasn't how this worked.

"Miss Steel, are you sure? Did you perhaps take a blow to the head? You cannot be thinking clearly. You said you wanted to be a virtuous virgin until the day you died, or until you reached your marriage bed. I remember it very well. You said…"

She waved a hand in the air. "Forget what I said. I'm sick of society and all the stupidity it asks of me. Of both of us. Right now, I want to celebrate being alive by doing the one thing everyone tells me I cannot do…while at the same time, trying to force me to do it. I wish to feel your manhood inside me, Sean.

Tonight." She blew out an exasperated breath. "Oh, I want to feel more than that. I want you to…do things I do not even know the words to express. What kind of world do we live in that I do not know the words for parts of my own body? You can sense my desires, can't you? You put them into words for me."

Yes, she most certainly did desire what she was asking for. He'd rarely felt anything so strong. And there was no guilt beneath it. She wanted sex with him.

But the words for what she wanted…things she had never experienced, nebulous desires winding their way through her mind of things overheard or glimpsed, but never completely understood.

Sean took a deep breath. "As your paramour, you wish me to make love to you. You wish to open yourself wide to me, so that I might thrust deep into your slick heat, stroking your tight inner walls until I drive you to the pinnacle of pleasure, and you anoint me with your essence, crying out my name to Heaven itself. But you desire for me, too, to share your pleasure, and so I must continue, thrust after thrust, until we both reach the peak of our pleasure together, and only then may I rest, before we make love again."

Miss Steel's face had gone quite red. "But you didn't tell me any of the names of the parts."

"Ah. Possibly because the words are vulgar, not usually the language of a paramour."

"How would you say it, then? You, Sean Bell, hellspawn and demon of Hell, currently my protector. If you wanted to do all those things to me, how would you say it?"

Sean swallowed. She had asked, and he must answer. He could lie, but…he felt she deserved honesty. "What I want is to sit you down, spread your legs, and taste your sweetness, so that I remember that there is still sweetness in this world. Then I want to hear your cries for joy, because I know I'm the cause of them. And then, when the time is right, I will seize the moment to take your virginity, but not your innocence, trading one pleasure for another, until you cry for joy again. Only then, when I know you are truly ready for me, would I dare to do as you desire. To drive my cock so deep into your dripping cunt, pounding into you as you scream for joy, screaming my name, over and over until you can think and feel and want nothing and no one else. And only then, when you have come for me countless times, will your pleasure be equal to mine, and we shall reach that peak together. Afterward, you will lie breathless in my arms for a time, before you beg me for more. And I will fuck you all over again, thrusting my rock hard cock into your hot, wet cunt…"

"Stop, please, Sean," she begged.

He bowed his head. "Forgive me, Miss Steel. I should not have…"

She shook her head. "No. Stop talking.

Sit me down, so we can start. Start…fucking."

The word sounded so dirty and delicious on her virtuous lips. Sean grinned. "And what would you have me do first, Miss Steel?"

SIXTEEN

Her voice came out breathless. "I want you to…sit me down, and pleasure me with your mouth and your fingers, until…until…"

"Until your cunt is dripping wet with want for me," Sean whispered, his eyes shining in the dark. He lit the lantern, then set her down on the bed.

She shrugged out of her waistcoat, then peeled off her pants, trying to wrap her tongue around the words.

"I want you to fuck my cunt with your tongue and your fingers, until I'm so wet with need for you, only your cock could possibly satisfy me," Carline said. She couldn't remember the rest, for Sean was already kneeling between her thighs, lifting her legs over his shoulders, as he bent his head to lap at her.

She let out a wordless cry as his tongue went to work, and again as his fingers speared into her, one, two, three. By the time he'd coaxed her to her second orgasm, she could think of nothing else but his body, and what it was doing to hers. Everything she wanted. Everything she wanted, and more.

Carline could feel her third orgasm building under Sean's relentless strokes. So close…so close…

"Tell me again, what you want me to do," Sean said, slowing down.

"I want you to fuck me!" she cried, trying to rub harder against him so that she'd tip over that approaching cliff. So close! How could he torture her so?

"With my fingers and my tongue?" he demanded, starting to pull his fingers out of her.

"Yes, yes! Don't stop!"

"What else do you want?"

She was nearly blind with want, so close to an orgasm and yet not close enough. "Fuck me, Sean! Please!"

So   close.

One…more…stroke…Carline exhaled,

ready to take a deep breath so that she might scream for joy. Sean's fingers spread her wide as they slid out of her and she let out a little "oh!" of disappointment at the loss, before hot, hard heat took their place, gliding deeper inside her than his fingers ever could, and she realised his thumb was still firmly pressed against her clitoris, slowly circling until…

"Sean. Oh my God, Sean!"

She clenched down hard, but the heat between her legs only seemed to swell in response, so waves of pleasure coursed through her, relentless as the sea, until she lay panting on the pillows, and she could see the ceiling of the tent again, and Sean's face, grinning down at her.

Her legs were still hooked over his shoulders, but his hands were now planted on the bed on either side of her, and when she looked down…

As if to tease her, he pulled his cock out of her, her eyes widening at the size of what had been inside her, glistening in the lantern light, before he glided back in again, that glorious heat rubbing against her insides just as he'd said it would.

"Tell me what you desire, Miss Steel," he whispered as he taunted her with another deliciously slow thrust.

"You," she said, then realised he was waiting for more. "I want you to fuck me until I scream, and then fuck me some more."

"As you command," he said.

SEVENTEEN

Morning found Sean with Miss Steel wrapped in his arms, his cock hard and ready for when she woke. She must have felt him stir, for she reached for him, fingers wrapping around his length as she tried to pull him inside her.

He entered her from behind, reaching

around to thumb her sensitive nub in rhythm with each thrust.

Her little moans of delight drove him on, one of the sweetest sounds he'd ever heard. Second only to when she screamed his name, and he'd hear that, too, before he withdrew.

Hell, she felt good. Like her body had been made for him, and him alone, it felt so perfect wrapped around him. Last night, she'd gifted him with three orgasms of his own, and he was well on his way to another already.

A quiet click sounded behind him, out of place in Miss Steel's tent.

Sean glanced back, to find the barrel of Miss Steel's rifle aimed at his head.

"Get off my sister," a soft voice growled.

"Sean, oh, Sean," Miss Steel moaned,

unaware of her brother's presence. She was close, already tightening around him, and Sean was loath to stop before she was satisfied. Especially if her brother was about to part them, perhaps forever.

"I said…"

Sean picked up the pace. Almost, almost…

"Oh, God, Sean, yes, yes, YES!" Miss Steel screamed.

Reluctantly, Sean withdrew, drawing the bedclothes up to cover her blissful body before grabbing his own trousers.

"Get out." The rifle tapped Sean's head.

Sean scrambled into his pants and out of the tent, his heart aching at the look of horror on Miss Steel's face.

EIGHTEEN

"Explain why I shouldn't just shoot you now," William said.

No – he couldn't shoot Sean. Carline wouldn't let him. She scrambled to find some clothes, wincing at the delicious ache from their lovemaking. If her brother shot Sean, she was going to search every spell there was until she found one that turned William into a frog, and she'd practice and practice until she succeeded at it.

Boy's garb was faster to don than any of her gowns, so it was in breeches and a shirt that the emerged from the tent to confront her brother.

"Answer me!" William demanded, poking Sean with the rifle.

Carline flew to put herself between them. "William, you can't shoot him!"

William glowered at her. "After what I just saw in there, it should be you shooting him."

Damn society and its stupid rules, for denying her such pleasures until she was a slave to her marriage bed. Unless…

"You can't shoot him because I'm

going to marry him!" she declared. "We'd already be married, if you'd come home sooner, but Sean wanted to wait until you could be at our wedding."

"That didn't look like waiting to me. It looked like…"

Ha, William was lost for words. Either he didn't know the right ones to say, or the only ones he did know weren't suitable for his sister's hearing.

"Sean came to keep me company and protect me after the attack. He knew I was frightened to be all alone here. A good thing he did, because the mill caught fire, and we barely made it out. I wouldn't have made it at all, but for him. He saved my life, William, and it seemed only fair to offer him board and lodging while he was here. And seeing as we only have the one bed…" Carline trailed off.

William still looked like a thundercloud. Nothing she said was going to calm him down.

"You truly wish to marry him?" William asked.

She wanted to stay with Sean and share his bed for the rest of his life. What were a few vows to that effect? "Of course," she said.

"And you? What's your name?"

Sean shot a questioning glance at Carline, but he answered William: "I'm Mr Sean Bell, a general labourer, come over with Mr Peel. Ask Captain Ellis, he knows all about it."

"So you have a land grant?" William persisted.

"Not yet, but he is entitled to one, so

I'm sure he will have one soon. Especially with a wife to support," Carline said.

"Why do you want to marry my sister?" William demanded.

"Because we're in love," Carline snapped.

William flapped a hand at her. "Silence, woman. I didn't ask you. I asked your prospective husband, and if his answer does not satisfy me, then I might still shoot him."

Carline's heart leaped into her throat. If it came to a fight between Sean and William, she knew who would win. William had never killed a man in his life and Sean…

"Mr Steel, I presume? Well, sir, if you need to ask, then you scarcely know your sister at all. A braver, more kind-hearted woman I have never met, in all my days. There are precious few women in this colony, and though I have not known Miss Steel very long, I immediately knew she was one of the most precious jewels womanhood has ever known, and I mean to make her mine, before any other man might lay claim to her."

Carline's jaw dropped. She quickly closed her mouth before her brother could notice.

"Well, then." William blinked, looking torn, before he firmed up his jaw and continued, "I'll just go across the river and fetch the Reverend, then, shall I? The sooner I see you two married, the happier I'll be." Without another word, he strode off toward the millpond.

NINETEEN

"Are you sure you want to marry me?" Carline asked, looking up at Sean. "I don't want to feel like it's an order or anything. Marriage is supposed to be something you agree to do freely."

Sean grinned. "I'm already bound to be your protector and paramour, for as long as you or I live. A few words said in front of some man who claims to represent God will not change that. And if it means less chance of your brother shooting me, or interrupting us while abed, then the sooner we say the words, the better."

Carline nodded slowly. Yes, she could see the logic there, but she'd always thought marriage should be something one did for love, not logic.

"It's just that…I never thought I'd marry a man to satisfy society."

Sean grasped her shoulders, and gazed deep into her eyes. "Did you summon me for your own desires, or those of others?"

"Mine, I suppose, but I meant to summon a protector…"

"Did you invite me into your bed to

satisfy your every desire, or because society demanded it of you?"

Carline laughed weakly. "If society knew I'd shared a bed with a demon, they'd hang me or burn me, for sure. No, I…I shared my body with you because it was what I wanted, and I believed you wanted it, too."

"So, is this marriage for society's sake…or what you want, Miss Steel?"

As she gazed up at him, her body still aching from last night's glorious lovemaking, she knew her answer. "I want you, Sean. I want you to protect me, to stand beside me in a fight, to help me dispose of the bodies of anyone who dares threaten us, and afterwards, I want you to fuck me so furiously I forget there is anyone else in the world except you and me. For as long as we both shall live." She swallowed. "And you should probably call me Carline, seeing as I'm about to become Mrs Bell, and not Miss Steel any more."

"With pleasure." And the look he gave her was filled with such smouldering heat, Carline feared her drawers might catch fire. Their wedding night couldn't come soon enough.

Reverend Wittenoom arrived sooner than expected, for William had met him halfway across the river, already on his way over to warn him about some ruffians who'd been threatening the other mill owners – sailors from a ship only recently come to port.

Carline, now dressed in her Sunday best, joined hands with Sean in front of the Reverend.

After an exchange of vows – with

Sean grinning as Carline vowed to obey him – and a quick wedding breakfast of cold mutton and bread William had brought from York, the Reverend was soon on his way again.

While Sean was distracted in helping the Reverend push his boat out, William drew Carline aside. "You must give up this witchcraft, now and forever, if you wish to keep your husband. For if he catches so much of a whiff of such things, you can be sure he will either beat you or leave you, or maybe both. You won't be able to dress as a boy any more, or shoot, or do any of the things I permitted you to do. You must be a good, obedient wife, if you want him to stay and protect you. Perhaps it is a good thing he has already had you – he knows you are biddable in bed, always a good thing in a wife. I won't take you back if he leaves you, Carline — I swear it. With a new mill to build here, Shenton and I will scarcely have enough money to feed ourselves through the winter. You and Bell will have to see the Governor about his land soon, for a man who eats as much as Bell surely does will be far more than we can afford. On the morrow, he must go. You tell him. Tonight you may have the tent, but tomorrow…he must go."

Too tired to even begin enlightening her brother, Carline simply smiled and nodded, then went to bed, where Sean kept her too busy to care for anyone else but him.

TWENTY

Carline patted her slightly rounded belly as she headed outside to draw water from the well. She wasn't sure what to expect from a half-human, half-demon baby, but Sean didn't seem worried, so she busied herself about the cottage Sean had built for them, extending the vegetable garden, and learning the names of her neighbours, who all seemed to know her name already.

"Mrs Bell?"

Carline glanced up, to see a girl scarcely out of her teens standing at the gate. "Yes?"

"Mrs Bell, my name's Sarah. Sarah Thomson. My husband and me, we're new to the colony. We lost all our children to the sickness and he thought…a fresh start, somewhere new, might help…" She sniffled, and the tears started to flow.

Carline patted the girl on the back, and invited her in for tea. As she set the kettle on to boil, Sarah's story came out. She'd tried to conceive more children, but they'd died, too, and they'd sought out the help of a witch, but it hadn't helped.

"I heard you might know a little about such things, and maybe, just maybe, you could help…?" Sarah's eyes were wide with hope.

What the girl needed was a foundation offering, of the fertility variety. Not as gory as the immortal protectors who could be raised by the full power of a foundation sacrifice, but the spell did hold power, nonetheless. "Do you have anything belonging to one of your late children? A shoe, or item of clothing, or favourite toy, perhaps?" Carline asked.

"We have a pair of little Tommy's shoes. They were a gift from his godmother. He never did grow big enough to wear them…" Sarah dissolved into tears again.

Carline dished out tea and comfort, along with some scones she'd baked that morning, and settled on a price for performing a witch blessing on the Thomsons' new cottage.

Sean would be proud — she earned almost as much as he did, now word had gotten around about her talents. Contrary to what William had always told her, witches were just as wanted here as they were back home. Especially a witch whose spells actually worked, as Sean well knew.

While Sarah prattled on about her husband's plans for his small block of land, Carline's thoughts drifted to the men she'd killed, and the foundation sacrifice ritual she'd almost completed, if not for William's interference. One day, she'd have to find out where he'd buried them, and finish the ritual. Stanley and Grant Steel, and the other two, whose names she didn't know yet. Four immortal protectors would be handy to have around the house, especially with Sean so busy with his own work now. He had a reputation as the strongest man in the colony, and everyone wanted his help with their building projects. Sometimes he came home almost too tired to make love to her. But only almost.

Yes, it would be nice to have more help around the house, so she'd have more time to spend with Sean. One day…

ABOUT THE AUTHOR

Demelza Carlton has always loved the ocean, but on her first snorkelling trip she found she was afraid of fish.

She has since swum with sea lions, sharks and sea cucumbers and stood on spray drenched cliffs over a seething sea as a seven-metre cyclonic swell surged in, shattering a shipwreck below.

Demelza now lives in Perth, Western Australia, the shark attack capital of the world.

The *Ocean's Gift* series was her first foray into fiction, followed by her suspense thriller *Nightmares* trilogy. She swears the *Mel Goes to Hell* series ambushed her on a crowded train and wouldn't leave her alone.

Want to know more? You can follow Demelza on Facebook, Twitter, YouTube or her website, Demelza Carlton's Place at:

www.demelzacarlton.com

More Books by Demelza Carlton

<u>**Colony: Aqua series**</u>

Halcyon (#1)

Poseidon (#2)

Apollo (#3)

<u>**Colony: Nyx series**</u>

Fang (#1)

Claw (#2)

Talon (#3)

<u>**Siren of Secrets series**</u>

Ocean's Secret (#1)

Ocean's Gift (#2)

Ocean's Infiltrator (#3)

<u>**Nightmares Trilogy**</u>

Nightmares of Caitlin Lockyer (#1)

Necessary Evil of Nathan Miller (#2)

Afterlife of Alana Miller (#3)

Romance a Medieval Fairytale series

Enchant: Beauty and the Beast Retold

Dance: Cinderella Retold

Fly: Goose Girl Retold

Revel: Twelve Dancing Princesses Retold

Silence: Little Mermaid Retold

Awaken: Sleeping Beauty Retold

Embellish: Brave Little Tailor Retold

Appease: Princess and the Pea Retold

Blow: Three Little Pigs Retold

Return: Hansel and Gretel Retold

Wish: Aladdin Retold

Melt: Snow Queen Retold

Spin: Rumpelstiltskin Retold

Kiss: Frog Prince Retold

Reflect: Snow White Retold

Roar: Goldilocks Retold

Cobble: Elves and the Shoemaker Retold

Float: Enchanted Horse Retold

Steal: Forty Thieves Retold

Call: Pied Piper Retold

Fall: Scheherazade Retold

Feather: Swan Maidens Retold

Curse: Rose Red Retold

Cross: Billy Goats Gruff Retold

Weave: Rapunzel Retold

Claim: Puss in Boots Retold

<u>**Heart of Stone series**</u>

Broken Chains

Broken Bonds

Broken Dreams

<u>**Heart of Steel series**</u>

Stone Guardian

Stone Champion

Stone Sentinel

Stone Shadow